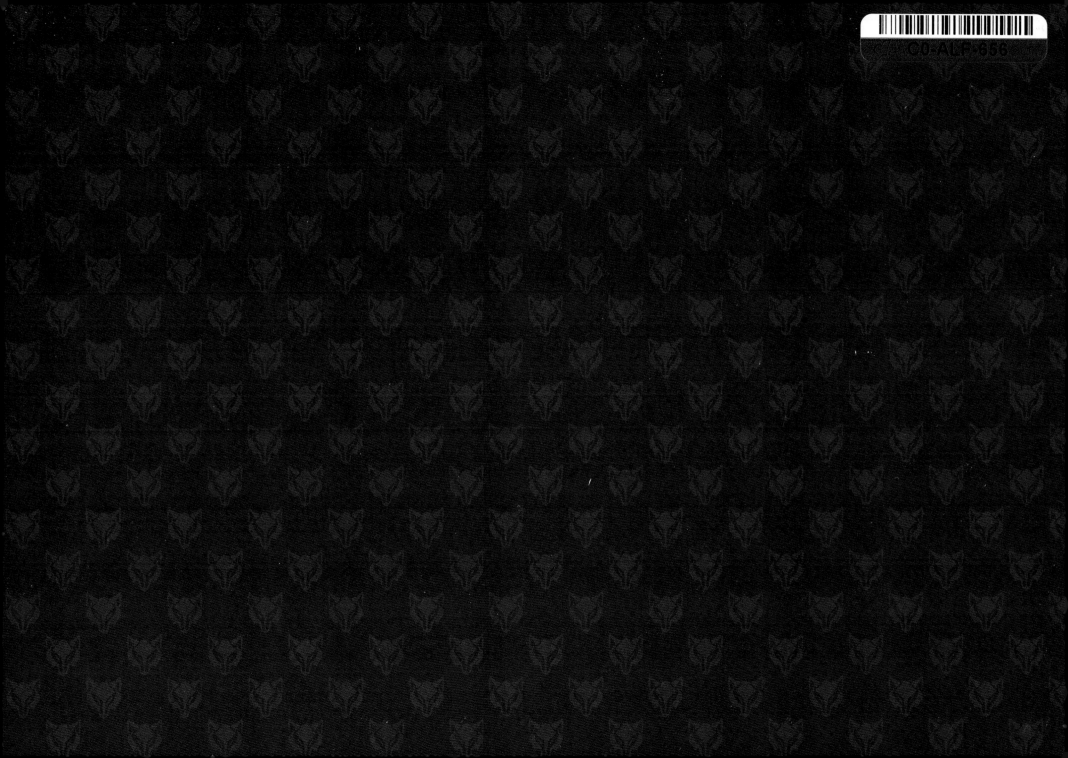

ISBN: 978-87-998176-0-3

Published by MOOD
Nytorv 17, 3. Copenhagen. Denmark

First edition: April 2015

Layout by Mathias Stilling Ambus .

Special thanks to Line Bundgaard and Iulian Drug for the tremendous effort
in producing Fall of Gods.

Printed and bound in Belgium

www.moodvisuals.com

Visit **www.thefallofgods.com** website to see more, or follow us on

our Facebook Page **facebook.com/sonsofmuspel**

Story by

RASMUS BERGGREEN & MICHAEL VOGT

Written by

MICHAEL VOGT

Illustrated by

RASMUS BERGGREEN

Additional artwork by the MOOD team:

JAN DITLEV

JONAS SPRINGBORG

TOMMY KINNERUP

SIMON FETSCHER

EVE VENTRUE

Table of contents

JOTUNHEIM

The harsh northern regions of the norse lands, inhabited by wild jotnar tribes.

JOTNAR

Intelligent sapient race, stronger and more instinctive than humans but lacking in certain mental faculties such as abstract thought.

MIDGARD

The southern regions of the norse lands, inhabited primarily by humans.

AESIR

An immortal race who once ruled the norse lands but have long since disappeared from the world. Worshipped as Gods by humans and as ancestors by jotnar, no one alive knows what they were or where they went.

THE RESERVE

Fenced in area established during the uprooting. The reserve is a peninsula covered in forest, inhabited by the forest Jotnar, known in human tongue as Faunir.

ELDEST

Primordial beasts who roamed the land while early humans hid in caves. The Aesir are said to have defeated and imprisoned these powerful beings.

Chapter One

HUNT

H O M E

She's gone.

Even before I call out, I know. As I stand in the doorway, hunting bow still in hand, snowflakes melting and dripping from my brow.

I know because the light has left. The strange light that turns a house into a home. And just as the truth sinks in, the next thought arrives. Sharp and cold and focused.

My wife is gone - and somebody took her.

THE TRAIL

Whoever did this was an old hand.

There are no signs of a struggle. Not a drop of blood. Nothing but a few subtle clues. A partial boot print. A whiff of cheap arrow grease, the kind used by the bandits and horse thieves who sometimes roam the countryside.

Most people would have bought it. Taken pride in how observant they were.

I am not most people. I can smell them. The men who were actually here. The soldiers. I follow their scent and sure enough - a subtle trail through the snow, all but concealed. Someone went to great lengths to cover their tracks.

Now most people around here are farmers. Not hunters, not warriors. Certainly not trackers. Which tells me two things. One, the people who took my wife are not from around here. Two, this was not random. They knew exactly who they were taking.

And more importantly, who they would be running away from.

MAGNAR

Magnar. If Freyja's face is the first thing I remember, his is the second.

During the Uprooting, Magnar led a successful campaign against a tribe of feral jotnar, pushing them deep into the wild unexplored woods. Then he raised a great big fence to make sure they stayed there. The Reserve, we call it.

Magnar seized the moment. Became chieftain of Drangavik, the largest city in eastern Midgard. They say he's well-liked. Guess few people know him as I do.

Magnar Asgarsson. My commander. My father-in-law. For all his talk of order and civilization, he did not act very civilized when his daughter fell in love with a nameless thug. Even one with my unusual set of skills.

The first time he came after us, seven men died. His men. The second time, it was worse. In the end, he let us go. Maybe it was sentiment, maybe something else. Freyja and I did not stick around long enough to find out. For fifteen years, he let us live our lives.

So what has changed now?

THE TAKEN

Dusk. I reach a small settlement by the edge of the woods. Drangavik people who got tired of Magnar's taxes and relocated back to the wild. Freyja and I came here last solstice and danced until the beer ran dry and the musicians keeled over from exhaustion.

These are good people. Farmers and woodsmen. They don't deserve this.

Everyone here tells me the same story. Someone has been taking the young. The strong and the beautiful. Twelve in all, over the course of weeks. Young men and women vanished without a trace.

A woman claims that free jotnar are to blame. That this is all Jotunheim's doing. Retribution for taking their land and enslaving their people. I understand her bitterness. The Uprooting was supposed to change things. Make people safe. To subdue the more primitive jotnar and drive out the dangerous ones - the clever ones with minds too close to ours - would bring order to the land. Give humans space to breathe, to build and to dream.

That is what chieftains like Magnar told us. But nature abhors a vacuum and chaos has a way of slipping back in.

An old man clutching his grandson curses the gods. The immortal Aesir. Those distant perfect beings who could do so much but choose to do so little. Me, I never pray. Freyja does sometimes, but me never. I do not like debts.

A cry goes up. A triumphant, hateful cry. The settlers have found someone to blame.

RELEASE

When I make it through the crowd, the flames are already crackling.

The jotun slave is big. Eight foot two and wider than any man, his skin like cracked aurochs leather. Jotnar folk are many things. Some are scarcely more than animals. Others have language and art and look to the night sky in wonder. This one's skull is flat and oblong and his eyes are dull. He must have belonged to one of the deep cave tribes.

The jotun howls. Tugs frantically at the ropes. They found him by the river, quietly eating a horse. Its rider had been bludgeoned to death with his own leg. None of the settlers care that the big dumb brute had an arrow lodged deep between his shoulder blades. Probably the rider attacked first. Still, this is not about justice. This is about blame. About release.

The jotun sees me. His dull mind recognizes sympathy in a sea of hate. His eyes beg me to stop this. How could I? Convincing these scared wounded people that this poor bastard did not kidnap their children would be like talking down a thunderstorm.

No. I cannot save the jotun, but I can ease his pain.

I wait until the flames reach high enough. Until the smoke makes the crowd squint. None of them notice the tiny dagger leave my fingertips and slip silently into the jotun's muscular neck, severing his brainstem. His head slumps forward. His pain is over. The crowd feels powerful for a little while longer.

Everybody wins.

P A N I C

For the first time, I am truly afraid.

I was sure about Magnar. So sure that I never even considered other possibilities. Still there have been rumors. I remember now.

There's a town, across the border in Jotunheim. Utgard. They say it began as a refugee camp after the Uprooting but then it grew. It evolved. They say the chieftain there likes to keep human slaves and whenever there is a demand, men will rise to meet it.

Slave-runners. Is that what has happened to the village young? To my wife?

I try to push it away. The panic, the pictures; Freyja, price tag around her neck, name and dignity stripped away, bartered like a sack of grain. No. Freyja, throat slit, her life ebbing into the bright snow. She tried to overpower her captors, could never tolerate injustice and she paid with her life. No. Freyja, hogtied and gagged, on the ground, as dirty pungent slavers sample their goods. NO.

My stomach turns to knots. I empty it violently against a tree. Nothing but bile, acidic and yellow. I cannot remember when I last ate. Focus. I push the fear away. Deep down into the dark well along with the rest of my past. Fear is for later. For now, there is only the hunt.

FROM BELOW

Too late, I realize my mistake.

I was so consumed I never even noticed where the tracks led me. We do not come here after dark. We all know the stories. Know what is lurking in the tunnels beneath the clearing. Beneath those smooth standing stones covered by long forgotten runes.

I can hear them, whispering below. Small leathery bodies scampering toward the light.

I met a völva once. A jotun witch, old as the fields. She claimed that humans and jotnar evolved from a common ancestor. That all living things are separate branches on the same tree. But if this is true, the shapes bursting through the frozen earth around me shot off eons ago.

The creatures are thin and scrawny, their skin slick and black, and their eyes a radiant blue. People say they dig into their victims, devouring them from within. Corpses have been found. Husks. Bags of skin with nothing inside, like dismantled scarecrows.

They watch me, unblinking. Their small sinewy bodies poised, taut like arrows. My inner hunter tells me to stand my ground, pound my chest and roar as loudly as I can, but these are no ordinary beasts. Theatrics will not fool them. Their eyes are aware and I can almost hear their thoughts:

You are big but we are fast. You are one and we are many...

I am running before I even know it. The world shrinks to a tiny orb. The creatures flank me, scurry up my legs and arms, a moving blanket of teeth and claws. I tumble headfirst and a thousand needles pierce my back.

Then a familiar sensation engulfs me. Something I have not felt for a very long time. I growl, clench my fists - and everything else fades away.

F I R S T   S I G H T

How long has it been?

I stand in a circle of dead jotnar warriors, blood steaming on the cold ground, and through that carnal mist, I see a face. A young woman. My hands drip. I look like a mad man. Yet she does not turn away. She stares at me with a mixture of horror and gratitude.

I know right then that I will love her for the rest of my life.

A second face appears behind her. A man. Older. Fierce and brash and boisterous. The kind of man who loves a fight, who leads from the front, but age and joint pain have slowed him down. I begin to discern what has happened. The young woman. Her father, an important man. Ambushed by the jotnar now lying dead in the mud. I saved them, but how did I get here? This woman, she brought me back. I know this truth, deep in my bones. But back from where?

I feel the ghost of a memory lingering just out of reach. Coarse thick ropes tightening around my wrists, neck and ankles. A flash of pain and a searing white single-minded, all-devouring rage. Then the memory fades and my questions along with it.

In the distance, a host of horsemen approach. Soldiers. Someone is fighting a war. The young woman's father extends his hand. "We could use a warrior like you", he says. I ask what they are fighting for. "The future", he responds.

To a man with no past, it seems as good a cause as any.

I open my eyes and see white clouds. For a second they look like wolves.

I am lying on my back. Somehow, it is morning. Something has torn the creatures apart, scattering their oily limbs all over the clearing. The carnage. The fury. It reminds me of that day. My moment of birth. Standing in the mud, my hands dripping with jotnar blood. Seeing my wife's face for the first time.

Freyja insists that I came out of nowhere, as if sent by the gods. Others have made less exalted claims. Some people say I am part animal. That my mother must have lain with a bear or wolf or land spirit and something wild, something feral passed into me.

If I ever meet my mother I will be sure to ask her if that is true.

This being within me, I call it the Rage. My animal shadow. We used to battle for control but for a long time the Rage has been dormant. With Freyja, I am calm, at peace. She is my lifeline, my rock. She saw something in me that no one else did. A light, a softness. She taught me how to chain the beast, but now the Rage has awoken. I can feel its claws

scratching against the inside of my skin and it scares me more than anything.

The Rage keeps me alive. It has put off my death more than once but I cannot lose control. I cannot allow it to overtake me again. If I do, my mind will slip back into the animal darkness from before that day.

And without Freyja to guide me, I might not be able to come back.

THE GREAT FENCE

The trail is lost.

During my blackout, my wife's captors moved too close to the city. They took a risk and it paid off. In the wild, their scent was like a beacon, but here everything smears. A useless blur leading in all and no directions.

The slavers will be taking Freyja north. Travelling by night, through back roads and hidden trails toward the Jotunheim border. I will need men and horses. Luckily, the city holds plenty of both.

Drangavik. Magnar's city. I made him a promise once. Now I must break that promise and ask for his help.

Here, on the edge of the city, I can glimpse the great wooden fence surrounding the Reserve. It has become taller since we built it. Maybe there was an escape? An attack even? Either way, I helped Magnar raise this wall. I locked up those wild creatures, turned their home into a prison and threw away the key.

CIVILIZATION

DRANGAVIK

I never liked this place.

Outside these walls, men live in packs. Inside, they live as a flock.

Civilization. A system in which people trade power for safety. This was Magnar's dream. For all his flaws, the man had a vision. Like his mentor Rolf Krake, the high chieftain who launched the Uprooting, Magnar Asgarsson dreamed of order. A landscape defined by lines on a map. A world tamed by fields and transformed by towns, where lights chase away the night and men take tomorrow for granted.

It was a potent dream. Easy to be caught up in for a man with no past, no memories, no opinions of his own. But progress has its victims.

Like the jotnar. I notice them at once. In a place so starkly human, they stick out like a sore thumb. These once wild hunters have become Drangavik's caste of servants and slaves. Meek and docile like cattle. A female jotun is heaving a huge sack of wheat on her sturdy back, obediently trailing after a ridiculous soft-bellied man. Another jotun is working

the anvil. His master yells drunken abuse, and then settles lazily in the shade with a bottle of mead.

Turning your back on a fully-grown male mountain jotun holding a forty-pound hammer is one of the most unnatural things I have ever seen.

One man's dream can be another man's nightmare.

G O D S

Gods. I did not expect them. I guess even city people need something to rally round.

The statues are made of wood and bronze. Awe-inspiring as they are, they are small against the massive Chieftain's Hall. The message is clear. Gods are more powerful than men, but the system is most powerful of all. Magnar has not lost his sense of detail.

I see one-eyed Odin, Allfather of the Aesir, a black raven poised on each shoulder. Thor, lord of thunder and war. Baldur, god of beauty, innocence and rebirth. There are many others but their names and function escape me. According to legend, the Aesir ruled millennia ago when ice sheets covered the north. Their world was young, wild and raw. Primordial beasts known as "Eldest", creatures of chaos and disorder, roamed the land while early humans hid in caves. The Aesir defeated and imprisoned the Eldest and paved the way for men and jotnar. Then they vanished and have been silent ever since.

Most men believe the Aesir were gods. Eternal and almighty, creators of earth and heaven. The jotnar are less impressed. They believe the Aesir were flesh and blood like us, mighty warriors once but now extinct. In other words, a waste of prayer. I think the jotnar have a point. Gods are a matter of perspective. What is the difference between gods and monsters? A god is just a monster you kneel to.

A small cough behind me. The guards who have been stalking me since I entered the gates make their presence known. They smell of mead, pork and a healthy dose of fear. Good. Magnar has not forgotten me.

AUDIENCE

Chieftain's Hall.

Naked girls sway gently like reeds. The air is heavy with the pungent scent of mushrooms. Magnar's eyes are glassy from the drugs. His hair has turned iron-gray and his tall, muscular frame is bloated. His chair can barely contain him. Victory has its price.

I get down on one knee. From the cave of my belly, the Rage stirs at the indignity. Fifteen years ago, I made Magnar a promise: to strangulate him if I ever saw him again. But promises are for honorable men and honor is a luxury I cannot afford.

I tell him everything. Magnar does not even flinch. I feel the Rage rising up. This was a mistake. This man will not help me. I am on my own. Magnar's lips are moving but I don't really listen. Something about a conflict in the Jotunheim borderlands. A group of human settlers massacred. High chieftain Krake has drained Drangavik of soldiers to teach the savages a lesson and Magnar can barely protect the city as it is. All the while, the Rage is screaming in my head. *Rip out his heart. Paint the walls in his blood and declare yourself ruler of the city. Then we will see how many men Drangavik can spare.*

I growl that we are talking about his only daughter. Magnar's voice grows harsh and bitter. His little girl died fifteen years ago and he does not intend to mourn her twice. I clench my fists, and from the shadows all around me hear the sound of bow strings tightening.

I know the location of each guard. I know who will fire first, second and third. I know who has the steadiest hand and who will panic. Only one thing stops me. Freyja. She taught me to see the world through the eyes of others. Not to treat people as objects. These young men have not wronged me. If I slaughter them to get to Magnar, if I tear them away from their wives, why should I deserve to reunite with mine? No. If I lose myself, I lose her.

The audience is over. I stagger toward the door. Through the red mist, I hear Magnar wishing me luck. I get the strange feeling that he means it.

I NEED ALCOHOL

I am losing control.

The Rage is clawing at the inside of my skull, throbbing in my temples. I need alcohol, as strong and foul as possible. Most men let loose their inner beasts when they drink, but for some reason, mine is calmed down.

I stumble toward the docks. Domain of drunkards, thieves and pirates. Street jotnar watch me with glazed eyes, clutching half-empty bottles. Theirs is a lost generation. Torn from their natural habitats, stripped of their dignity, Drangavik's new servant caste dull their shame with whatever plonk they can get their hands on. At least they remember what was taken. Their children will not. This here is all they will ever know. Freyja and I once saw a dancing bear at a village fair, dressed up in human clothes. The creature could easily have broken its chains and ripped every grinning spectator to pieces but the bear believed it was powerless, and chains of the mind are the hardest to break.

I approach the seediest bar in sight, trying not to think of how the distance between my wife and I grows bigger with every wasted second. With a trembling hand, I carve an X into the tether pole outside.

Whoever is watching will know where to find me.

THE AUROCHS

The place's name is The Aurochs.

City guards celebrate their end of watch, a pleasure girl on each arm. Human-jotnar pregnancies are rare but not impossible. We call the results half-breeds and most end up repeating the same pattern.

Across the room, a group of drunken anglers bawl an old shanty. Something about a great serpent lurking in the depths, waiting for the call of the wild. Everyone here is best friends right up until the moment the knives come out.

I take another deep swig of the bottle. The spirits settle in my bloodstream like a calm blanket of snow. The throbbing wanes, the Rage slithers back into its lair. I feel my mind going soft. It would be so easy to continue. To drink my mind into a pleasant numb stupor.

I push the bottle aside and wait. A minute goes by. Maybe two. For one unforgivable second, I almost rest my eyes. I think of my wife, of the time our little girl was stillborn. I wanted to tear the house down, unleash the Rage just to escape the pain, but Freyja - gods know she was hurting too - stared down the beast. Told me that pain is part of life. What counts is how you deal with it. She was always stronger than I was.

I jerk to attention as a young man appears at the back entrance. He looks like a merchant but the sword on his hip is Norfolk steel. A sword for fighting, not parading. He nods ever so slightly in my direction, then turns around and leaves the way he came. I tip the barkeeper and follow.

Magnar's soldiers are not the only organized faction in this city. Pirates have fast, silent ships and use a system of flares to send coded messages up and down the coast at incredible speeds. With a little luck, these men can pick up the slavers' trail. The question is what they will ask in return.

AMBUSH

Dusk is upon us. The wind is cool on my face and the air smells of algae.

Five men are waiting in the alley, backlit to obscure their faces. Even so, something is wrong. Their posture, their stance. Pirates are like thieves, they move like birds. Fast, jittery, alert. But these men move like wolves. Mercenaries. The door slams shut behind me. Then someone speaks my name.

I was afraid this might happen. Whether I like it or not, I used to be famous. The bear man, possessed by a wild spirit. Furious, merciless, unbeatable in battle. Plenty of free jotnar would pay handsomely to see my head mounted on their wall, not to mention the rivals of Magnar that I helped strip from power. Fifteen years have passed, but Freyja says my face has not aged a day.

I draw my axe. It drops to the ground. My hand feels like lead. Only then do I feel the tiny sting at the back of my neck. The young man from the bar somersaults over my head and lands like a cat. In his hand, a small blowpipe. Damn it. A hundred daredevils in this city and I get the one crew smart enough not to fight honorably. A dozen tiny needles. Expertly placed. The paralysis will last for only a few moments, but I doubt they plan to give me that long.

Their leader steps forward, draws a saw-toothed blade. Freyja's smile explodes in my mind.

A wet thud. The leader jerks. A slender arrow has entered his ear. He looks puzzled as he drops. The men gasp. A shadow moves behind the sails of a nearby ship and another man falls to his knees clawing for breath, a jotun throwing weapon coiled tight around his neck. Everyone draws their weapons and forms a circle. No one notices my fingers twitching, my head starting to turn.

My axe is in the air. Three left. I catch the sword of the man whose face now holds my axe. The sword is in the air. Two left. My elbow breaks a set of ribs and punctures a lung. One left. The young acrobat with the Norfolk blade. He grins, shifting his sword from hand to hand. Then a second arrow appears out of nowhere, piercing his knuckles. He winces but makes no sound, and in three impressive jumps, he is over the rooftops.

ISELIN

A figure descends the mast and jumps ashore. This one moves like a bird.

The woman is young, her hair brown and her face covered in freckles. She flashes me a cheerful grin, retrieves her throwing weapon and lays out the half-suffocated man with a kick to the jaw. All the while, she never stops talking. *She got my message. No one does X's anymore. I should really try to keep up. It was lucky she found me when she did.*

Her name is Iselin and she says that I killed her father. He had been one of the mercenaries Magnar sent to kill me when Freyja and I eloped. I vaguely remember a lazy-eyed thug with a taste for knives. He died badly. I ask Iselin why she would help me. She lifts up her shirt, revealing a row of deep old scars across her back. I see. Because I killed her father.

An alarm goes off in the distance. Reinforcements are coming.

We board Iselin's ship, weigh anchor and slip out of the dock. I never liked the open sea, but right now I'll take any friends I can get.

PRISONERS

The ship's name is Verdandi. Iselin named it after one of the Nornir, the three maidens of Destiny. It means, "that which is coming into being". In other words, the present. A fitting name for an outlaw.

We are at the ship's bow. In the distance, Drangavik's lights fade as the fog wraps itself around us. I have not eaten or slept in days but sleep can wait. Because something strange has been happening at the Reserve.

Rumors speak of masked men leading chained prisoners through the main gates in the dead of night. Very cloak-and-dagger. The one city guard who shot his mouth was found face down in the river.

Iselin believes this is where the slavers took my wife. The Reserve. Not Jotunheim.

My head is spinning. If Freyja has gone beyond the fence, Magnar could be involved after all. For whatever reason, someone is helping Reserve jotnar kidnap Midgard citizens. The question is, dare I risk everything on the word of a pirate girl I have only just met? Madness. Except, it doesn't feel like madness. Iselin might be an outlaw but she despises slavery. Her mother was a slave. I believe she wants to help. Besides, the irony is too perfect.

I used to be a monster. Me, not the Rage. The Rage is just a beast and to be a monster you need a conscience. You need choice. The truth is I killed because they told me to, because I could. I was stupid, proud and arrogant. I did horrible things and I have been running away ever since, but eventually, everyone must pay their debt.

I built a prison. Now I am breaking into it. How our useless gods must be laughing.

THE RESERVE

The Reserve emerges from the fog.

The fence itself is impenetrable. Sixty feet tall, made of giant oak trunks, with archer towers guarding the only entrance. Yet, the Reserve is a peninsula and three of its sides border to the sea. Jotnar do not swim but even if they did, escape was never a concern. A maze of ragged rocks lie between the coast and us. An unforgiving stretch of whiplash waves and treacherous currents that only a fool would attempt to navigate.

Iselin's crew eats currents like this for breakfast. At least, so she tells me.

The dark waves crash hard over our heads. I pretend not to notice as a jagged rock grazes the hull with an ear-splitting crunch. The steersman just shoots me a toothless death-defying grin. He is a free jotun and his shoulder bears the "brand of the Eldest". They say a new jotnar religion is being born in cities all over Midgard. A faith for the downtrodden, identifying not with the Aesir but with their conquered enemies.

Aesir and Eldest. Men and jotnar. Order and chaos. Is history repeating? Freyja once told me that time is cyclical. The

present returns to the past, retroactively changing the past. Whatever that means. My eyes tend to glaze over whenever my wife tries to teach me the finer points of the cosmos. Still, if the present alters the past, what does that say about a man with no past at all?

There is another thump against the hull. Softer this time. I look over the stern and catch a glimpse of a bloated leathery body. Then another and another. The sea is littered with corpses. As I said, jotnar do not swim.

So the question is: what would make them desperate enough to try?

TROLL

Dawn. The coast is barren and lifeless.

Stretching out ahead of me, the Reserve. The last unmapped territory south of Jotunheim. Tall cliffs and thick pine forest for countless miles. We confined our enemies to this harsh place for a reason. No man wanted to claim it. I follow a narrow ravine going inland as Iselin's ship disappears on the horizon. She was certain we would meet again. She is a child of civilization. It must be good to have such faith in tomorrow.

I know the smell even before I see the bones. That fat oily fur, sickly sweet.

We call them trolls. They used to be part of our collective nightmares. Hunters would bang their shields when crossing a rock bridge and farmers drew circles of ash around their staples and granaries. All children once knew that trolls are short-sighted, and young men would prove their courage by standing in a dark cave entrance, counting to ten with their backs turned and their eyes closed. That was before Magnar and the other chieftains hunted trolls to the point of extinction.

This one could be the last of her kind. I do not want to hurt her. Besides, Freyja would kill me. She has always despised her father's belief in human supremacy, his insistence that all other races are expendable in the quest for progress. I need to think fast.

R O C K S L I D E

The troll leans in close.

She sniffs the air and exhales heavily. Her breath is indescribable. If I move a muscle, she will see me. Slowly, I glance upward. There is a loose boulder on the cliffside above us. A rockslide waiting to happen.

I wait until the sun is in her eyes. She squints, turns away, her huge horns almost brushing the tip of my nose. Then I drop, roll, throw. The troll jerks, grunts, her eyes zeroing in on the movement. Her pupils dilate. She sees me. Then - above us - a deep rumble as my axe finds its target, sending rocks cascading down the cliffside. A boulder hits her square on the forehead. She stumbles, stunned but not out. I leap, sprint between her great legs, dodging rocks big enough to crush me, and charge toward the trees.

A disappointed roar and a whoosh of air. I duck as something large hurls pass me. The dead stag explodes against the rocks, a blast of blood and bone and entrails. Of all the deaths I've evaded in my time, being crushed by a flying deer ranks with the best of them.

I pick up a sharp piece of broken antler and head into the forest.

A wild weapon for a wild place.

Chapter Three

WILDERNESS

THE FOREST

In the wild, the stars are closer.

Out here, the canopy of the great world tree stretches across the sky and the stars are fruit upon its branches. In the city, stars are simply other worlds like ours, adrift and alone in an infinite void. Some of the philosophers even claim that the cosmos is in a state of flux. That the stars are only real because we are here to watch them.

The mind of man at the center of creation. A Midgard idea if ever I heard one.

My raft cuts through the murky river. I have travelled upstream for the better part of a day. I reach the river's source, a clear spring gushing down from the mountains. I breathe in deep, close my eyes and feel every leaf tremble with the forest's dark heartbeat. This must be what Jotunheim is like. Raw and alive.

Midgard and Jotunheim. When did we start to think like this? Before the Uprooting, the land was just the land, but draw a line on a map and something emerges on either side. Something with a heartbeat of its own.

I wade ashore and start looking for tracks. My heart is pounding with the thrill of the hunt. The Rage is writhing, alert and on edge. It too feels the wildness of this place. It fills my mind with pictures. Fantasies of revenge, savage and sweet. I push it deep down, order myself calm. I want to slaughter these jotnar for what they have done but they are too many, too fast and too dangerous. Finding my wife is all that matters.

FAUNIR

This was always their land.

Jotnar of the deep woods. Tree-dwellers wrapped in cloaks of bark and moss, adorned with antlers, tusks and claws. Men called them the faunir, or simply "green folk".

Before the Uprooting, people would sometimes meet them at the edge of these woods and trade skins or meat for trinkets and ornaments. They were shy but curious. Drawn to art - tattoos, patterns and drawings - even if their minds could not grasp its purpose or meaning.

When Rolf Krake and his allies came to rid Midgard of the jotnar, this tribe held their ground. They dug tunnels and laid traps, fading in and out of the trees like deadly green ghosts. A thousand men lost their lives in these woods. Some were dragged underground, their lungs stuffed full of dirt. Others were strung from treetops by their own intestines. The poison on faunir knives would make vines grow inside you and squeeze your heart until it burst, or erupt from your mouth, nose and ears until you choked.

Morale got low. Magnar changed tactics. He pushed the tribe as deep into the woods as he could and walled the whole area up. Problem solved. Technically not a victory but Krake was impressed. Magnar became chieftain of Drangavik. For fifteen years, segregation has been the law of the land. Until now.

Did Magnar take part in this madness? Did he tell his men to abduct his own daughter and hand her over to his enemies? If he truly did, it will not matter why.

Certain lines you do not cross.

WALKING IN CIRCLES

I am walking in circles and for every lapse, I feel myself grow dimmer. The woods seem to curve in on themselves. Infinite but only from the inside. Soldiers used to call it "tree blindness". Some thought it was magic. Like people need help to get lost.

I pass the same clearing for the third time. The same dying campfire. The same human tracks leading into the heart of the forest. My wife was here and yet I cannot track her. Useless. My skin is prickling, my eyes itching from the murky air, heavy with unfamiliar pollen and spores. These woods were always unfit for humans. Too wild, too much like Jotunheim.

An unseen bird follows my every move. I hear it chirping whenever I cross my own tracks. A spiteful gloating sound lively with anticipation. A countdown. I pass the clearing a fourth time and now I feel I am being watched. Shapes are emanating from the trees, always in the periphery of my vision, moving only in the blind spots.

The Rage is stirring. As I grow weaker, the leash loosens. It tells me to let go. Give in to the wild. I clasp my hands over my ears in a futile attempt to drown out what is already

inside. I cannot let it overtake me. Not now, not here. I know in the deepest, oldest reptilian recesses of my mind that if I let go in a place like this, I will never claw my way back into the light. There will be no Freyja this time. No miracle awakening. I will live out my days as a dumb animal, oblivious to what I once was, what I could have become.

I stagger through the underbrush like a growling, panting madman...

...and then I see the boy.

THE MUTE

The boy is young.

His skin is gray and soft, almost human. Not yet the cracked leathery gray of a mature jotnar. His cloak is a living blanket of moss, and a pair of boar tusks, almost comically big, hang from his scrawny neck.

He is afraid, yet he never cries out. Unsheathes a little stone knife with trembling hands and tries to put on a brave face. I look at the splintered, bloodied antlers in my own hand. This boy is a faunir. His tribe has kidnapped my wife but right now I am just too relieved to see a familiar creature and this one is harmless. I lower my weapon. The boy understands the gesture. He approaches me, launching into a sequence of hand gestures and grunts. He is a mute, but his eyes are bright and clever.

He notices my blank expression, grabs a stick and writes a single word in the soft mushy ground: *Prisoners.* I nod. He continues: *Rune Mountain. Village. Follow. Eyes down.*

The boy tugs urgently at my hand. I follow sheepishly, eyes to the ground. Trust the earth, not the trees. Clever. I notice that the Rage is silent. No shadows move at the corners of my eye. There is only our footsteps and the boy's warm reassuring grip as soft moss gradually turns to hard rock.

For the first time in days, I feel strangely calm.

TRAP

They call it Rune Mountain.

Ancient symbols scar the rock face as if carved by some superhuman force. The place must have been important to the Aesir, but its significance has been lost to the ages.

The faunir village lies near the base. Ramshackle huts built into the trees. Once it must have been charming. Now, eerily deserted. We approach upwind so they will not smell us coming. The jotun boy points toward a strange structure. It takes me a moment to realize what I am looking at. A giant wolf made of branches, and at its feet, a string of cages. Cages with people inside.

I creep toward the empty square. The village is completely still. Yet with every step, I feel a chill return to my bones. A nagging doubt. Something is very wrong here. What was the boy doing in the woods and why would he betray his own people to help me? Why has the Rage gone silent in my head and, more alarmingly, why did I not ask these questions before? I look at my hand. My palm prickles from the boy's touch. Suddenly I understand. The faunir are medicine men. Their weapons are organic. The pollen I inhaled, making me paranoid. The boy's touch, a herbal toxin; the same that keeps Magnar's serving maids blissfully docile, compliant. Trusting.

This is a trap, and I have blundered straight into it.

VÖLVA

The ground opens up beneath me.

There is a sharp pain and the impact knocks the air from my lungs. High above me, antlered faces peer over the edge of the pit. Strong vines slip around my arms, legs and neck. I am reminded again of that ghost of a memory, the sensation of being hanged. Then the jotnar hoist me from the hole.

Their völva touches my forehead, leaving behind a smear of red paint. Two cruel eyes adorn her ceremonial robes. I see that she recognizes me, senses the animal shadow inside me. Still her smile is one of grim relief, not triumph or glee, and she reeks of fear. In fact they all do. Something is very wrong here.

My captors drag me toward one of their cages. I call out my wife's name but the choir of my captors, hooting and chirping like birds, drowns out any reply.

ELDEST

My companion is young.

He has an infected gash across his eye, the lid swollen tight. He wears the banner of Drangavik on his battered coat. One of Magnar's soldiers. I ask him what happens to the prisoners and he recounts an impossible tale.

In the bowels of Rune Mountain, a creature has awoken. A colossal wolf held in place by magical chains. The jotnar believe it is an Eldest, one of the primordial beasts who roamed the frozen world eons ago before the reign of the Aesir.

When its howl first split the night and its shape stood black against the stars, there was great awe and wonder. Then came the petrifying terror as the jotun tribe realized the gravity of their situation. For the first time, they felt the walls of their prison, trapped inside the Reserve with a monster. An ancient predator threatening to burst its feeble chains and devour everyone in its path. They began by sacrificing their old, sick and dying to sate its ravenous hunger, but to

no avail, and in their desperation, the jotnar turned to their greatest enemy.

Magnar saw at once the danger to his city and chieftainship, should the great wolf break free. He appealed to Rolf Krake for assistance but the conflict in the Jotunheim borderlands occupied all of Midgard's army. Magnar had to buy himself some time. He ordered his most trusted men to kidnap young men and women from the countryside, offering them up as fodder for the beast. However, the wolf only grew more ravenous.

Magnar turned to superstition, as desperate men do. He became convinced that only royal blood would appease an Eldest. His beloved son and heir Sweyn was out of the question but there was another one. The one who left. The one who rebelled.

The daughter who broke his heart.

THE DUEL

We emerge from our cage, squinting in the pale afternoon light.

The jotnar tether me to a pole, cut my companion's ropes and place a sword in his hands. Then they stand back in grave anticipation. The young soldier rubs his wrists, too ashamed to look at me. On his last slave raid, he took pity on the prisoners but the jotnar caught him trying to aid their escape. This is his punishment. Honor or not, he will do what he must to survive.

The soldier is well-trained. He does not rush. Comes toward me slowly, deliberately. I am unarmed. His range exceeds mine. He can stay in the periphery, bide his time, wear me down until I make a fatal mistake. The Rage is silent in my head, still dulled by the herbal toxins but I have one advantage. I am not well-trained. I do not fight fair.

I feel something sharp lodged in my side. A piece of the broken antler. Must have happened when I fell into the jotnar's trap. I pretend to slip in the mud, to lower my defenses. The soldier takes the bait and strikes. I dodge and ram the splinter through the hollow of his knee. He screams,

I lunge and head-butt him, break his nose with my elbow as he buckles over. The rest is routine.

An eerie sound erupts from the crowd. The jotnar have seen enough. A rope materializes from out of nowhere, jerking the young soldier into the air. He twitches for what feels like an eternity, then goes limp. They cut my tether and a spear jabs me urgently in my back. I do not object. I know where I am going. The soldier thought the winner would go free, but I know better. The strong make the best sacrifices.

I am going after Freyja. According to the young dead soldier, they took her only moments before I arrived. I can still make out the prisoners' tracks in the wet mud. I am close now. She only has to stay alive for a little while longer.

WOLF'S LAIR

The mountain rises out of the fog.

I can just make out a huge black portal in the rock face. A door to the hidden cave inside, exposed by a recent earthquake. My jotnar escorts halt, chirp fearfully at me to proceed. They have armed me with the dead soldier's blade. A sword against a monster. Jotnar humor perhaps.

I step deeper into the fog. The smell and the warm damp air is unmistakable. This is a slaughtering ground. I feel something crunch beneath my feet, like seashells after a flood. Kneel and pick up some bone fragments. Human bones. I feel a surge of panic and the Rage snaps awake inside. I must be out of reach of the jotnar toxins. Then something catches my eye amidst the bones. A glint of gold. I do not even notice picking it up, but suddenly the object is in my hand, unbearably, pitilessly real. My wife's brooch.

The world drops away. As hope dwindles, my mind clutches at straws. She could have dropped it, could be hiding somewhere between these rocks. The Rage knows better. *What did you expect,* it jeers.

Did you think you were charmed? Favored by the gods. Did you believe the world was fair? That because you fought and bled and never gave up, you would be rewarded? Think again. There is no fairness, no justice. Only mindless chaos. Time to let go.

I sense the shadows shift and something emerges from the mouth of the cave. Tall as trees and gray like a winter sky. Silent but for its slow heaving breath, like a gust of hot wind, and the soft jingle of a chain. The wolf looms over me like an impossible dream. Beautiful and terrifying. I cannot hope to fight it. Not unless I allow the Rage to overtake me. Fine. Death or oblivion, either one will do. Freyja would not want this, but I no longer care. My wife is dead. I will follow her into the dark but first, I will have my revenge.

I turn and face the beast. Its eyes are wells of immortality and in their reflection I sense the chasmic depths of time, dizzying, pitiless, and inhuman. Then I let go. The Rage crashes over me like an angry wave and everything goes soft.

THE PACT

She is gone. I am here. Somehow, I am still here.

A memory teeters right at the edge of consciousness, only part my own:

In that last moment, when we stood before the wolf, the Rage and I were one. Indivisible. My hatred fused with sadness. Compassion for the great beast, chained for so long in the dark. I knew then that the wolf was a force of nature, beyond right or wrong, no more to blame than disease or a thunderstorm. But the jotnar, they were accountable. These cruel cowardly savages and their conspirer Magnar, the swine who sacrificed his own people, his own daughter, to save his worthless crown. Those were the ones who were going to bleed. Every single one of them. I remember bringing my sword down hard on the wolf's chain. Aesir steel. Light as a feather and stronger than anything in the natural world. No man should have been able to sever it, but I was never just a man.

The wolf bowed its great head. A pact was made.

I stagger back through the fog, guided by the screams and horrifying roars. When I reach the village, it is already over. The destruction is total, the carnage beyond belief. Houses ripped apart, torn limbs scattered like leaves. A small body, much too small, is face down in the mud, crushed by a giant paw. That is when I realize what I have done. From deep within comes a cold mocking voice. *Is this not what you wanted?*

A dead silence falls over Rune Mountain and in the distance, an ancient creature howls at the moon, joyful and reborn.

SOLE SURVIVOR

My wife is gone.

How long before it truly sinks in? First was the numbness. Then came the dull throbbing. Soon the pain will burst through my skin like icicles.

For a long time I walk among the corpses. Then I sense movement. Someone has survived the massacre. A small scrawny figure huddled in the darkness of a narrow cave. The mute jotun boy. He is shaking all over, surely traumatized. His family gone, his elders, everything he has ever known. An entire culture, wiped out in minutes.

They were only trying to survive. What would I have done in their place?

We stare at each other for a while. Does he know what I did? Does he understand why? Perhaps he is wiser than I.

Perhaps he understands that we have all been the victims of a perfect storm.

I drop the dead soldier's sword and walk away. The jotun boy hesitates, and then begins to follow me from a safe distance.

I don't object.

Chapter Four

PYRE

DEVASTATION

I see the smoke from miles away.

I tell myself it will not be so bad. Drangavik is strong. Civilization has thick walls. Besides, the pact was for Magnar, no one else. Except in my fury and despair, at one with my animal other, I forgot why Freyja taught me to chain the Rage. It sees people as things. As obstacles, and the wolf is no different. It is immortal. It was here when nature sparkled with magic, before the glaciers receded and the land turned green. To it, we are nothing but clever ants.

There is a gaping hole in the fence surrounding the Reserve. Tree trunks ripped from the earth like weed. That is when I hear the screams. Of pain, shock, and despair.

The wolf has carved a trail of destruction through Drangavik. A few houses are on fire, some are rubble. Wide-eyed citizens head for the safety of the woods, carrying nothing but their wounded and the clothes on their backs. Their words are frantic, fragmented, but they tell me all I need to know. Reinforcements had come at the very last minute.

Courageous Drangavik soldiers returning from the front succeeded in driving away the wolf.

Magnar is wounded, but he lives.

I will pay for my mistakes. For Freyja, for the lives lost in my wake, but debts are for later. For now, I have a promise to keep.

RETRIBUTION

I descend from the roof of Chieftain's Hall and slip in through the window.

Magnar is slouched on a bed, draped in furs, a bloody bandage around his head. He turns his head, eyes glassy, long drunk to ease the pain.

He lets me know what I have done. What I have started. Rolf Krake will use this to his advantage. He will blame the jotnar for awakening the wolf and rally all of Midgard against Jotunheim. He has waited years for a chance like this. Magnar only did what he had to. Sacrificed a few to protect the many. He is not lying. He believes he made the right choice and he would do it again. All men do right in their own eyes. That is when I realize. Magnar did not sacrifice Freyja because of superstition and folk magic. This was always about me. Magnar needed a champion to defeat the wolf. The legendary bear man, possessed by a wild spirit. But he knew that I had learned to control the Rage, leashed it and buried it so deep that only a tragedy would release it. Like the death of my wife.

He does not resist when I put my hands around his neck. We both know this is what needs to happen. Magnar dies

on his back, without honor or grace. It is better than he deserves. So why does he smile toward the end, smug and triumphant?

Why does it feel like he won?

THE LEAP

I shut Magnar's eyes.

That is when I sense someone watching me. The young man is poised in the doorway, his handsome face contorted in anger. Freyja always said that one day her little brother would be a great leader. The kind of leader Midgard really deserved. He only had one flaw. He was blind to those of his father.

Sweyn Asgarsson releases his bow. I stagger back from the impact, arrow stuck between my lower ribs. The second arrow hisses past my ear. Behind Magnar's only son, angry shouts and the pounding feet of approaching guards.

The room is too small and I am unarmed. I have only one chance. I turn, pain throbbing in my chest, and make a dash for the window. I leap headfirst into the night as a third arrow slams into the back of my thigh.

Then there is only the wind and the dark water below.

BURIAL

I drift for what feels like ages.

For a time I have a mind to go under, to sink like a rock and be swallowed by the sea, but no. I do not deserve death.

A scrawny arm grabs me by the collar and drags my tired beaten body ashore. The mute boy shivers, shaking off the icy water like a dog. Jotnar folk are afraid of water. This must have taken all his courage. We exchange a silent nod. He deceived me in the woods. Now we are even.

We hide underground while I dress my wounds, until the search parties give up. Then we emerge and I drag myself toward the trees. The boy follows. He has no reason to. I guess when you are lost, any direction will do. Or maybe he simply doesn't want to be alone.

I cast one last look at Drangavik. Out in the fjord, Magnar receives a hero's burial. The pyre lights up the black waves, then the ship goes down. The creator is dead but the creation lives on. I know now that Magnar was living in fear. Not of the wolf, but of the monster he made. The truth about civilization, Magnar told me, is that once set free it can never be controlled. In the wild, time is a circle. You know the future by observing the past. But here, time

is an arrow pointing in only one direction. Forward, always forward. The Aesir defeated their ancient beasts, but we have made a beast of our own and its hunger is insatiable.

I turn my back on the city. I know what I must do. I failed my wife. I failed the man I fought so hard to become. I let the darkness win, the chaos and the wilderness. Now I must bear the pain, contain the damage, chain what I unleashed. I need to catch the wolf.

She told me that pain is part of life. What counts is how you deal with it.

I guess we will have to see about that.

To be
CONTINUED

THE NOMAD

While his host sleeps, the nomad reaches out.

He knows all the shortcuts, the pathways through the roots that connect all living things.

In Drangavik a band of mercenaries set off to hunt down their chieftain's murderer. In far away Jotunheim, the refugee king dreams of war machines. And all over the lands, the Eldest begin to awaken.

The nomad is elated. It has begun. It took him years to summon the magic, spread thin across this bleak unspectacular age. But he dropped a pebble into the lake and now the rings are spreading. He recalls the vision he received so many years ago, in a cave beneath the world where the first men drew their pictures.

Soon, man will hide in caves again. Time will reset.

All will be right with the world.

Creating the

UNIVERSE

A NEW TAKE

The Norse mythology has always been part of the Scandinavian story tradition, and even though we don't recall all the tales, every Dane, Swede and Norwegian know about Thor and his hammer, the monstrous Fenrir and the beautiful Freya - Not to mention the jotnar; the Scandinavian counterpart to giants and trolls.

The stories are very dramatic and, like most pagan myths, there is little distinction between good or evil, which I find very inspiring. Instead, they are about outsmarting your opponent, stealing something important or getting someone to love you. Even the gods feel fear, jealousy and love. They are like humans, only more powerful and (sometimes) wiser. These stories teach us a morality and worldview that is quite different from today and transport us back in time.

As a kid, I loved the "Valhalla" comic books by Peter Madsen and the novel "Erik Son of Man" by Lars-Henrik Olsen, both of which did an excellent job in depicting the world of Norse mythology for a younger audience. Now, Hollywood shapes the contemporary perception of the Norse setting and for a while, I have been curious about why there has not been a serious attempt to make an authentic Scandinavian version of the Norse setting for a mature audience.

Would it not be great if someone took inspiration from this fantastic legacy and created a Norse universe with a distinct Scandinavian voice? A story that embraced the inherent brutality of the world, the awe-striking nature and the ambiguous morality?

I shared these thoughts with Jan Ditlev, my friend and co-founder of our studio MOOD, and together we produced some foundational sketches. We both felt we were on to something exciting - something that might also inspire others. Not long after I convinced writer Michael Vogt to join me, and suddenly I did not only have pictures, but also words accompanying and challenging them. Our work rapidly condensed into a unique fantasy; not the Norse tales re-told, but a brand-new world inspired by them.

We wanted to depict a world where the gods were once real, but have long since faded from the land. An "alternate history" Scandinavia, marred by racism, imperialism and war, where two intelligent races inhabit the same space and civilisation is starting to reshape the destiny of the Nordic tribes. Last but not least, we wanted to create an anti-hero protagonist who tries to do good, but is cursed by a violent past. We pair the epic with the personal, and we value the good story over action and the fantastic elements in order to create a world that feels real, grounded and captivating.

We have developed Fall of Gods as a mini-series. Book 1 is a hard-boiled tale, inspired by Film Noir and classic westerns and focuses on personal loss and revenge. We love how this seems like a "local" story, tied together by Magnar's betrayal. From here on the universe will rapidly expand in scope, and become more complex and rich on characters, as the stakes are raised and more of the old magic and mythological elements creep back into the world. Soon our nameless warrior will face even bigger problems and we cannot wait to continue telling the story.

As we tried to imagine this world, we quickly realized that not many books looked like ours. We are somehow in between a graphic novel, an illustrated book and a novel. We have strongly tried to embrace this and use it as a strength, so that story and illustrations supplement each other on every spread. I have always wanted to make such a book, where the illustrations were part of the storytelling, and not just pretty pictures.

I knew from the beginning that I wanted to have a strong cinematic approach to underline the reality of the world. I present the illustrations as snapshots of the scene, composing my images as a cinematographer on set, looking through a lens. With this Art Direction, I have tried to give the images more life, and I hope that it will enhance the feeling of a real world with real emotions, and feel less like a typical fantasy world. Part of this approach is also to embrace the imperfect; the grey weather that makes the picture less epic or a blurred character, caught too close to the camera. The most important thing to me is the immersion of the reader.

I have included some sketches that I think are fun to look at and tell a bit about the process. Usually I start out by making multiple smaller sketches to try out different angles and ways to communicate the story. I wanted to sketch out the whole book as fast as possible, to see how the images fit in context and order. When I felt the sketch worked, I started my painting layer. The whole art direction is semi-realistic, and I have drawn upon matte painting techniques, to give it this dimension.

I hope you have enjoyed the book. We most certainly have loved creating it.

-Rasmus Berggreen

COMPOSITION

Starting out, I try to think about how to convey the story by making several smaller sketches like the one you see here. I think about composition and whether the story is easily perceived.

Norse mythology is filled with drama, and I try to incorporate this into my art. For this piece I had been studying lava formations and how this extreme condition creates a lot of steam. I began imagining creatures materialising in the steam which inspired me to paint this fire giant; bulky, heavy and with lava as blood..

SHAPE AND COLOR

Next I think about the silhouettes of the creature and the man, and the overall colours. To make the creature scary, I need the shape of it to feel dynamic with a strong silhouette.

I roughly paint in the colours, using a brush that has a good flow and roughness to it. I already know I want the ground and the dark lava rock to contrast strongly, so I try to work with the balance, creating an almost overexposed look in the process. I also look at lava references, and find the orange shades I like.

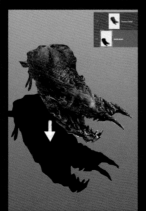

APPLY TEXTURE

To achieve the semi realistic look, I need to apply texture to my image. I found I can control the process well by making a black silhouette of the object I want to apply texture to, and keep a separate layer on top with the texture. Then I would always be able to edit in the actual shape without deleting from the texture.

I never just make one texture, I follow the shapes and think about how shadows and highlights would react to the lighting. This gives it a three dimensional look. When I am happy with the amount of detail, I add fog on top and I am just about done.

RASMUS BERGGREEN

Born 1980 in Denmark. After graduating from the The Royal Danish Academy of Fine Arts as a production designer, he worked in the Games Industry as a concept artist on the Hitman series, developed by IO Interactive. In 2013 he started the visual development studio MOOD, along with three fellow artists. As part of the team he helps clients evolve their brands.

MICHAEL VOGT

Born 1980 in Denmark. After taking a master's degree in Film & Media Science at the University of Copenhagen, he was part of the artist group Good Boy! Creative. In 2012 he joined IO Interactive as a dialogue writer on "Hitman: Absolution". He is currently the main writer on the upcoming sixth installment in the Hitman franchise.

THANK YOU

We want to show our gratitude to all kickstarter backers. Your help has been invaluable.
Thanks to you, we have been able to invest all our hard work into creating this world. Also,
we want to thank each of these individuals for making an exceptional contribution:

Abel Ang · Aaron Mason · Alan Callihoo · Alexander Motlagh · Alexandra Dictovny · Allan Saunders · Anders Hove Christensen · Andre Nedderman · Andrew Gray · Andrew Musick · Andrew Solomon George Raeymaekers · Anne Draaisma · Benjamin Bock · Bree Waldron · Brian Nielsen · Christopher Coleman · Christopher McLennand · Christopher T. O'Brien · Cliff Winnig · Cole Swinehart · Coniah Grimes · Corey Giesemann · Corey Nelsen · Curtis McGrath · D. Mertens · Daniel Soh · David Baillargeon · David Grabowski · David Luong · David MacArthur · Edward Morton · Elliot Boyce · Elliott Crosby · Espen Skarsten · Estephano padron · Francisco Luna · Francisco Naranjo · Garrett May · George Golston · Gregory Bruneau · Ian Voglesong · Jack Windsor · Jacob Bartolini · James Ryan · Jason Peroutka · Julian Harper · Jesse McElveen · Joe Dean · Jonathan Chance · Joshua Alumbaugh · Joshua Doble · Juncheng Li · Karl Krueger · Kenneth Livitski · Kenneth Madsen · Kenny Magnusson · Kieran Densey · Klaus Berggreen · Kyle Tracy · Larke Galyan · Lars Christensen · Lars Rasmussen · Lucent Crow · Mack Busby · Martin Vaughan · Mathew Lorenceau · Matt Rochester · Matthew Papirnik · Matthew Swarbrick · Michael D Billman · Michael Rud Jakobsen · Michael Tandarich · Mikkel Høgh · Mikko Sinisalo · Morten Rask · P.E. Thomas · Patrick Patzer · Patrik Carlvik · Paul Rossi · Paul Thomas Smith · Paul Tobin · Peter Christian Risager · Peter Eide Paulsen · Philip Cahiwat · Phillip Ramirez · Rasmus Lindeberg · Ryan Coulombe · Sally Dominski˜ · Samantha Moglowsky · Sarah Stevenson · Sean Heffron · Simon Sams · Sven Hilm · Terrence Hannon · Todd Graham · Trent Bramer · Walt Dueck · Walter Simonson · Yel Legaspi · Yen-Yit Soo · Yu Hin Lam · Yuzhe Zhou · Zachary Arand